Ladybird  Readers

The Boy Who Shouted Wolf

Series Editor: Sorrel Pitts
Text adapted by Mary Taylor
Activities written by Catrin Morris
Illustrated by Masha Ukhova
Song lyrics by Wardour Studios

LADYBIRD BOOKS

UK | USA | Canada | Ireland | Australia
India | New Zealand | South Africa

Ladybird Books is part of the Penguin Random House group of companies
whose addresses can be found at global.penguinrandomhouse.com.
www.penguin.co.uk   www.puffin.co.uk   www.ladybird.co.uk

Penguin
Random House
UK

First published 2021
001

Printed in China

A CIP catalogue record for this book is available from the British Library

ISBN: 978–0–241–47555–3

All correspondence to:
Ladybird Books
Penguin Random House Children's
One Embassy Gardens, 8 Viaduct Gardens, London SW11 7BW

MIX
Paper from
responsible sources
FSC® C018179

Ladybird Readers

The Boy Who Shouted Wolf

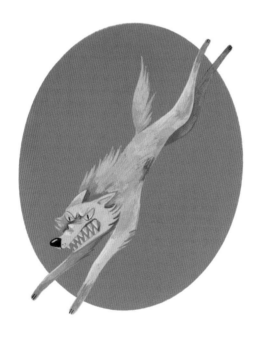

Picture words

Jack

Jill

father

mother

grandmother

the villagers

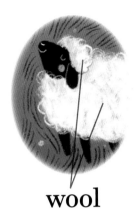

wool

knock

play tricks

wolf

tell a lie

tell the truth

Jack lived on a farm with his mother and father, his grandmother, and his sister, Jill. All the family helped on the farm. They worked hard, but they were happy.

There were fruit trees and a garden
where the family grew vegetables.
They had a cow, which gave
them milk.

They had chickens, which gave them eggs. In the fields near their farm they had lots of sheep, which gave them wool.

The farm was near a village.
The people from the village were
friends with the farmers and
their families.

They worked together in the summer.
They looked after the village in
the winter.

The children played together, and
there was always a big party when
young people got married.

Jack was usually a good boy, but sometimes he was naughty.
He loved playing tricks!

He knocked on people's doors and ran away. The people soon became angry, and Jack stopped knocking on their doors.

Jack played lots of tricks on his family.

He put apples and potatoes in Jill's bed. She was surprised when she tried to sleep!

One day, Jack sat down next to the cow and waited for his grandmother.

When she came, he said, "Hello," in a loud, low voice.

"Help!" his grandmother screamed.
"The cow is talking to me!"

One night, when his family were all asleep, Jack pushed grass inside their shoes.

In the morning, they were surprised when they got dressed!

"Why can't I put my feet in my shoes?" Jill thought.

"Are these MY shoes?" his grandmother thought.

"Are my shoes smaller today?" his mother thought.

"Are my feet bigger today?" his father thought.

One day, Jack's father asked him to look after the sheep.

"It is an important job, Jack,"
he said. "You must look after our
sheep, and the other sheep, too.
There are wolves in the hills.
They're dangerous! If you see a wolf,
shout 'Wolf!' and the villagers will
come to help you."

When Jack was watching the sheep,
he became bored.

He tried to have fun.
He sang.

He stood on his head . . . but he was still bored.

"I have an idea," he thought. "I am going to play a trick on the villagers!"

He put his hands to his mouth
and shouted.

"Wolf! Wolf! WOLF!"

When they heard "Wolf", the people all ran up the hill.

"Where is the wolf?" said Jack's father.

"There isn't a wolf!" said Jack, laughing. "I wanted to play a trick!"

"Don't do that again!" said
Jack's father. "If there isn't a wolf,
DON'T shout 'Wolf!'"

The villagers and the farmers all
turned around and walked back
down the hill.

"Jack is a naughty boy!" said a villager to Jack's father.

"He is usually a good boy," said Jack's father.

A few weeks later, Jack was bored again.

He ran after rabbits.

He climbed trees.

He threw stones . . . but he was still bored.

"I know!" he thought, smiling.

He put his hands to his mouth
and shouted.

"Wolf! Wolf! WOLF!"

When they heard "Wolf" again,
the people all ran up the hill.

"Where's the wolf?" said the people.

"I was playing a trick!"
said Jack, laughing. "There isn't
a wolf!"

Jack's family was angry. The people were angry. They shouted at Jack, "Never shout 'Wolf!' if there isn't a wolf. Never! Don't tell lies!"

"I'm sorry," said Jack.

The people all went back to
their work.

They were very angry with Jack.

"I'm never going to be naughty
again," thought Jack.

"Jack is a really naughty boy!"
said the villagers to Jack's father.

"I'm sorry," said Jack's father.
"He isn't going to do it again,
I'm sure."

A few weeks later, Jack was sitting on a wall, watching the sheep.

Suddenly, he saw a wolf! It was walking slowly and quietly towards the sheep. It was winter, and the wolf was hungry . . . very hungry.

Jack jumped on to the wall and shouted, "Wolf! Wolf! WOLF!"

In the village and on the farms, people heard Jack shouting, "Wolf!"

This time, they didn't run. "Jack is playing a trick again!" they said.

In the field, the wolf came nearer and nearer to the sheep. Jack shouted louder and louder, but nobody came to help.

The wolf jumped on one of the sheep. His mouth was open wide. The other sheep ran out of the field, far away.

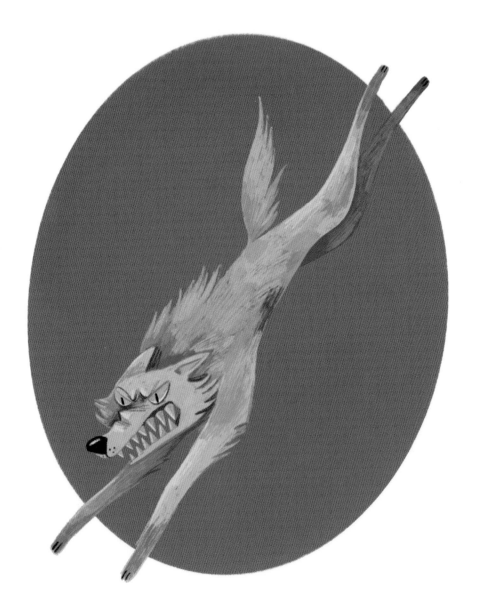

Jack ran down the hill to the village.

"Didn't you hear me?" he said. "Why didn't you come? There's a wolf up there! It has eaten one of our sheep! The other sheep have run away!"

43

First, people were angry
with Jack.

Then, they felt sorry for him.

"Jack," said his father. "If you tell lies, people won't listen when you tell the truth."

"I understand, now," said Jack. "I'm sorry."

45

Activities

The key below describes the skills practiced in each activity.

🖊 Spelling and writing

📖 Reading

💬 Speaking

🎧 Listening*

❓ Critical thinking

🎵 Singing*

✦ Preparation for the Cambridge Young Learners exams

*To complete these activities, listen to the audio downloads available at **www.ladybirdeducation.co.uk**

1 Match the words to the pictures.

1 Jack

2 Jill

3 father

4 mother

5 grandmother

6 the villagers

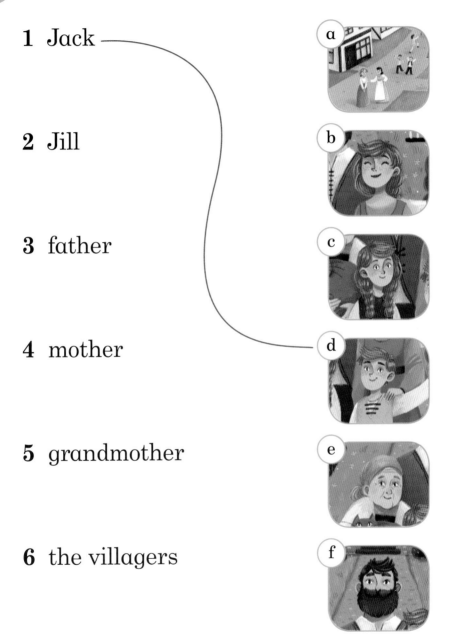

2 **Look and read. Choose the correct words and write them on the lines.** 📖 ✏️ ✪

> play tricks   knock
> tell a lie   tell the truth

1 Jack does this to people all the time.

play tricks

2 Say something that you know isn't right.

....

3 Say something that you know is right.

....

4 You do this on a door and people open it.

....

3 Write the missing letters.

th   an   ee   he   ol

1  fa .t. .h. e r

2  m o t .... r

3  g r .... d m o t h e r

4  s h .... p

5  w .... f

4 Circle the correct pictures.

1 You get milk from this.

  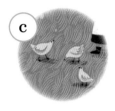

2 You get eggs from this.

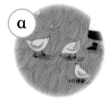 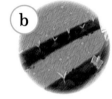 

3 You get fruit from this.

4 You get wool from this.

 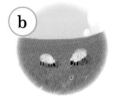 

5 Ask and answer the questions with a friend. 🗩 ❓

1

Describe Jack's house.

Jack's house is big and old.

2 Who lives in the house with Jack?

3 Which animals and plants do they have on the farm?

4 What is in the village near the farm?

6 Read the story.
Choose the right words and write them on the lines. 📖 ✏️ ⭐

1	between	near	under
2	after	from	with
3	at	in	on
4	after	for	out

The farm was ¹ .... near .... a village.

The people from the village were friends

² .... the farmers and their

families. They worked together

³ .... the summer. They looked

⁴ .... the village in the winter.

7 Circle the correct words.

1 Jack was usually a **bad** / **good** boy, but sometimes he was naughty.

2 He **hated** / **loved** playing tricks!

3 He knocked on people's doors and ran **away.** / **in.**

4 The people soon became **angry.** / **happy.**

5 Jack **started** / **stopped** knocking on their doors.

8 **Write the questions.**
Then, write the answers.

1 (did) (Jack) (lots) (of) (on) (play)
(tricks) (Who) (?)

Question: Who did Jack play lots of tricks on?

Answer: He played lots of tricks on his family.

2 (sleep) (did) (feel) (tried) (How) (to)
(Jill) (she) (when) (?)

Question: ....

....

Answer: ....

....

9 Who said this?

| Jack's grandmother | Jack | Jack's father | the villagers |

1 "Help! The cow is talking to me!"

said ___Jack's grandmother___ .

2 "You must look after our sheep,

and the other sheep, too,"

said _____ .

3 "I wanted to play a trick!"

said _____ .

4 "Jack is a really naughty boy!"

said _____ .

10 **Listen, and write the answers.**

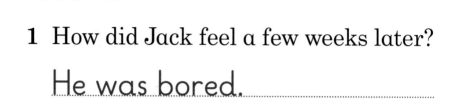

1 How did Jack feel a few weeks later?

He was bored.

2 What did he run after?

3 What did he climb?

4 What did he throw?

5 What did he say?

11 Talk about the two pictures with a friend. How are they different?

In picture a, Jack looks happy. In picture b, Jack looks sad.

12 **Order the story. Write 1—4.** 📖

.... Jack saw a wolf walking slowly and quietly towards the sheep.

.... Jack jumped on to the wall and shouted, "Wolf! Wolf! WOLF!"

.... Jack shouted louder and louder, but no people came to help.

......1...... Jack was sitting on a wall, watching the sheep.

13 **Circle the correct sentences.**

1  **a** The wolf came nearer and nearer to the sheep.
b The wolf ran far away.

2  **a** The sheep jumped on the wolf, and it ran away.
b The wolf jumped on one of the sheep.

3  **a** Jack ran down the hill to the village.
b Jack ran up the hill to the sheep.

14 Write about this story.

....

....

....

....

....

....

....

....

15 Look at the pictures.
Tell the story to your friend.

1

2

3

4

5

6

> *Jack and his family lived in a house near a village . . .*

16 Look and read. Write the answers as complete sentences. 📖 ✏️

1 Where is Jack?

He is in the village.

2 Who is Jack with?

....

3 Why is Jack sad?

....

17 Sing the song.

Jack and his family lived on a farm.
They had sheep and a cow.
They had friends in the village.
They all were happy now.

"There's a wolf!" shouted Jack.
"Where's the wolf?" they said back.
The people all came quick,
But it was a trick!

Jack was very naughty.
He really liked to play!
But if you trick and lie to friends,
they won't listen to what you say.

"There's a wolf!" shouted Jack.
"No, there isn't," they said back.
The people thought it was a trick,
But then the wolf came quick!

Visit www.ladybirdeducation.co.uk
for more FREE Ladybird Readers resources

✓ Digital edition of every title

✓ Audio tracks (US/UK)

✓ Answer keys

✓ Lesson plans

✓ Role-plays

✓ Classroom display material

✓ Flashcards

✓ User guides

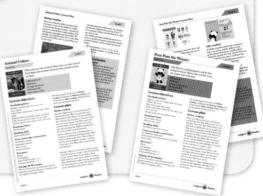

Register and sign up to the newsletter to receive your FREE classroom resource pack!

To access the audio and digital versions of this book:

1 Go to www.ladybirdeducation.co.uk
2 Click "Unlock book"
3 Enter the code below

5GRnmOojlT